PATHWAYS TO BOLINGBROOK

A BOLINGBROOK BABBLER STORY

BOOK 1

WILLIAM BRINKMAN

Praise for the Bolingbrook Babbler Stories

Pathways to Bolingbrook:

"Two smart women trying to survive in difficult times. *Pathways to Bolingbrook* captures your imagination and leaves you wanting to know what happens next. Can't wait for the publication of the novel. Well worth reading." — Amazon reviewer.

"This is a very short introduction to what is sure to be an entertaining series, if just for ONE THING: Iowa is not boring." — Amazon reviewer.

"Keep reading. Keep writing, Mr. Brinkman, and all the best with your Anti-Psychic Kitty Press. Breathlessly waiting for your next publication. Six stars!" — Amazon reviewer.

A Fire in the Shadows:

"A thrilling 'vampire' fantasy packed full of twists, turns – and danger!" — Wishing Shelf.

"This was a fast-paced and exhilarating supernatural and sci-fi YA fantasy! The world-building and mythos that the author built into this series were evident immediately." — Author This was a fast-paced and exhilarating supernatural and sci-fi YA fantasy! The world-building and mythos that the author built into this series were evident immediately." — Anthony Avina, author

"I have never read a book so fast before! It sucks you in from the very first sentence. I can't wait to read more books from this author." — Goodreads reviewer.

The Rift:

"A richly written novel filled with memorable characters. Highly recommended!" — The Wishing Shelf.

"A quick, easy and interesting read that had good writing, a good storyline and well developed characters." — Goodreads reviewer.

"Every new development in the story surprised me and -- there are weredeer!I don't usually read fantasy or sci-fi, but this book made me want to take another look at the genre. I highly recommend it!" — Amazon reviewer.

"*The Rift* is a wild adventure, sprinkled with humor, duplicitous characters, and extraterrestrials. You never know who is working for the good of mankind or creating a rift in the world." — Amazon reviewer.

For the latest news about William Brinkman and the Bolingbrook Babbler stories, subscribe at h ttps://bolingbrookbabbler.com/mailing-list

To my wife for her years of love and support as we've traveled on
our pathway.
To the residents of Bolingbrook for inspiring me over the years.

A BOLINGBROOK BABBLER STORY
PATHWAYS TO BOLINGBROOK
WILLIAM BRINKMAN

Contents

Anywhere is Better Than Here

MIRIAM SAT ON A wooden bench as the last drunk college students filtered out of the Pedestrian Mall. The soothing sound from the Pissing Sisters, the nickname for the tubular water-spouts atop of the fountain in front, failed to comfort her. Miriam knew it was only a matter of time before a police officer would chase her away, but her body felt too heavy to move. If she could move, she thought, where would she go?

"I didn't expect to find you here," said a man.

Startled, Miriam turned and saw Matthew, wearing a black blazer, black jeans, and a white t-shirt with an *IndustrialnatioN* logo on it.

Miriam turned her attention back to the Pissing Sisters. "Where should I be?"

"Lots of places. The House of Chaos—"

"Someone would post about it on ISCA."

"Hanging out with Tommy Stinson's new band?"

"Saw them back in 1992. Gabe's charged way too much to watch them rehearse, and Tommy didn't play any Replacements songs."

"Good point. But I still have to wonder—" Matthew sat on Miriam's bench and moved closer to her. "Why here?"

Miriam shifted away from Matthew, keeping her eyes on the fountain.

Matthew continued. "After all the effort to slip away from Pete and his associates, you end up here. Out in the open, with no escape."

Miriam sighed. Hours earlier, she'd escaped from Pete and his associates after a pointless argument. After running away to Iowa City years ago, Miriam eventually wound up in his circle. She knew Matthew was one of his out-of-town partners, but beyond a few polite conversations, and some dances, she didn't know much about him.

"There is no escaping Iowa City," said Miriam. She noticed herself touching her abdomen and quickly moved her hand away. "So I might as well be in my favorite spot, watching the sisters pissing the night away. So, if you're here to bring me back–"

"I took care of Pete."

Miriam gasped and faced Matthew. Matthew brushed back his medium-length blond hair.

"Took care of him?" asked Miriam, unsure if that was good news.

"Not like that. But you don't have to worry about Pete any-more."

Miriam didn't know how to respond. "Thanks, I guess." She looked down at herself. "Unless something changes, I'm always going to have to worry about him. The Emma Goldman Clinic isn't a charity."

"Family?" asked Matthew.

Miriam turned away and faked a laugh. "That's a joke." She felt a tear running down her face and brushed it off. "They threw me away years ago."

"Threw you away?"

"My dad got angry and tossed me out. The rest of my family went along with it."

"All of them?"

Miriam fought off her tears as she remembered her sister.

Matthew continued, "I can't imagine–"

"Do you want something?" snapped Miriam.

"Want?"

"Yeah. Do you want anything? Because I'm not in the mood for small talk. And I probably don't have what you want. So, if you want to get high, find a seller. I'm out of that. If you're hard up, there's a massage parlor near the tracks."

Matthew chuckled and gestured towards Miriam.

"That's what I want."

"What?"

"Think about it. Here you are in the Ped Mall, acting like you're about to be pushed off the edge of the world." Matthew jumped backward, performed an aerial somersault, and landed on the upper ledge of the fountain. Miriam was surprised he didn't stumble. Matthew looked down. "And oblivion is so tempting right now. No more pain. No more problems. Just eternal peace. All you have to do is stop resisting and jump." Matthew jumped up, performed another somersault, and landed inches from Miriam. "But you won't jump. Why? Because you're a fighter. Not one of those muscle-bound fools, but a real fighter. You fight because you know. You know death doesn't offer you peace. It offers you nothing. It turns you into a decaying lump of matter. It turns you into something as common as dirt. Yeah, life can suck, but you have to know that you're one of the lucky ones. You're alive, and you know that you're alive, and not only do you know you're alive, but you can also appreciate that you're alive, and you can appreciate the world around you. How many other collections of atoms can say that? Hmm? Not many, and on some level, you must know that. That's why you fight. You fight because this is your only chance to be sentient.

Every feeling is a gift. Sadness, fear, pain, pride. All things worth living for. On some level, you have to know that. That's why you fight. That's why you're fighting right now. You're standing on the edge, but you're not going over without a fight. That, Miriam—that's why I like you."

"You're weird," Miriam replied.

"I have been called many things, my lady." Matthew stretched out his arms and bowed slightly. "'Weird' is a title I accept with honor." He leaned back and lowered his arms. "I am weird, and I also offer you an alternative to oblivion."

"What?" she asked, expecting something unworthy of his flowery performance.

"I run a family business."

Miriam tensed up. "What do you sell?"

"We sell sustenance, but our mission is to change the world, one sale at a time."

Miriam gave him a skeptical look.

"For better, of course."

"Is it legal?"

"Technically."

"Technically?"

"It's legal in a court of law, but let's just say we have powerful competitors. The laws of men do not constrain them. That's where you come in. We need a scout, and you've already demonstrated your qualifications."

"By escaping Pete?"

"Much more than that, Miriam. I've heard so much about you and seen much more than you know. Joining the family would be perfect for you."

"You still haven't told me what your business does."

Matthew looked around. "We should discuss this in private."

"Let me guess, your place?"

Matthew shook his head then gestured towards the tallest building in Iowa City, a hotel. "Have you ever been to the top?"

Miriam shook her head.

"Want to go?"

"Seriously?"

"Yes. I can get us there. Follow me."

Matthew started towards the covered alley leading to Dubuque Street. After a few steps, he looked back at Miriam. "Unless you don't want."

Miriam looked at the fountains, then at Matthew. "No tricks."

"Not like that."

Miriam jogged to catch up to Matthew, who stepped into a dim portion of the alley. She started to talk, but he motioned for her to stop.

"You remember the last time we danced?" he whispered.

Miriam couldn't forget their slow dance. While the others were content with the prom hang, He held her at arm's length and tried, unsuccessfully, to get her to spin. She nodded.

"Remember our hug afterward?"

"Yeah," she replied. It wasn't that memorable, but it didn't seem creepy at the time.

"Let's hug then."

Miriam reached out to hug Matthew. When they embraced, darkness materialized around them like a cloud. In moments they were surrounded by total darkness.

"I got you," whispered Matthew as he tightened his embrace. She felt her feet rise from the ground and sensed that she was accelerating like she was on an elevator.

Miriam thrashed her legs but still couldn't feel the ground. "What are you–". The shadows dissipated, and Miriam saw that they were floating above the hotel roof.

"Oh my God!" she gasped.

"Not so loud."

They gently floated down to the roof. Matthew released his embrace. Miriam stumbled back, almost tripping over her feet.

"How—How did you do that?"

"Magic," said Matthew. He opened his mouth as he protracted two fangs.

Miriam staggered back at first.

Matthew retracted his fangs. "Yes."

"Yes?"

"Yes, I am what you think I am." Matthew pointed. "If this frightens you, the door is behind you. If you leave, know that you will never see me again."

Matthew turned his back to Miriam and strolled to the edge of the roof. Miriam watched him for a few moments as he looked out into the night sky. Cautiously, she approached Matthew. She noticed how his hair flowed in the occasional breeze and the almost perfect smoothness of his skin.

"What do you see?"

She stopped. "See?"

Matthew motioned towards the edge of the roof. "What do you see out there? Oblivion?"

Miriam hesitantly moved closer as she felt her fear of heights grip her. She felt chills as she neared the edge.

"You won't fall." He offered his hand. She grasped his hand, now noticing that her hand was slightly warmer than his. Miriam took a deep breath and crept closer to the edge. She looked down and instinctively tightened her grip.

"I've got you," Matthew replied. "You're safe."

Miriam caught her breath, but she kept a tight grip on Matthew's hand. She looked out at the Iowa City skyline. In the distance, Miriam saw the Old Capitol complex and the Van Allen Physics Building. She loosened her grip slightly.

"What do you see?"

She took in more of the view. Her fear faded. "I don't see oblivion. It's beautiful. You know, whenever I felt stuck, I'd look up at this hotel and imagine myself standing right here. I thought maybe I could see the way out."

"And now that you are up here?"

She paused. "I don't see it. I just see a small city in the middle of nowhere."

"You just have to know where to look. It's not a physical path. It's the possibilities that you have to look at."

Miriam turned her head towards Matthew. "Possibilities?"

"Yes. You see, centuries ago, the Mongol hordes were on the verge of conquering Europe. Europe's armies were no match for the Mongols' superior horsemen and tactics. Kingdoms that once seemed invincible crumbled before the invaders. It seemed like nothing could stop them from obliterating Europe. Think of it. Everything about Europe–Art, culture, literature, knowledge–all gone, trampled by the hordes.

"But in the shadows, a small group met in secret. They were determined to not only defend Europe but also to make sure that no nation, kingdom, or tribe could ever threaten it again. On what seemed to be the eve of Europe's destruction, they formed a pact and vowed to do anything, holy or infernal, to ensure Europe's security.

"Their first efforts were small but successful. They built on those successes and learned from their failures. When the pact shattered, their successors continued the work. Over time, European civilization grew larger and more powerful than the original conspirators dreamed possible. Because of their efforts, we are now standing on top of a building and looking out at a city built in the middle of nowhere. A city that came about because of decisions made centuries ago."

Matthew faced Miriam. "Join me, and I'll offer you a new life. Free yourself of your burdens. Free yourself of this place. Accept my offer of rebirth and I will help you discover your possibilities."

Miriam looked out at the Iowa City skyline again. She smiled as she looked past the lights of Iowa City and into the darkness. "Tell me more."

Think of the Children

Sara Langston noticed her publisher, James, marching towards her desk.

She spoke into her cellphone: "I have to go, Jacob, but I'll be home tonight."

"Okay," replied Jacob. "You won't forget?"

"I'll remember," Sara replied. "Because I always think about you. Goodbye."

"Goodbye, mommy." Sara ended the call and looked up at James. "I'm almost finished with—"

"We need to talk. In my office."

James immediately turned and started towards his office. Sara rose from her desk and rushed to catch up to him. As she did, she remembered when the *Star* newsroom was crowded with reporters. Most of them were still upset over the management's decision to downsize from four Chicago suburban bureaus. Now, half the desks were empty, and the remaining reporters now covered more than one community.

James pushed the door open and walked towards his desk. Sara stopped the door from closing long enough for her to enter.

"Sit," James said bluntly as he sat down.

Sara sat down, concerned about what was coming next.

James paused for a few beats. "The mayor of Bolingbrook says you're trying to arrange an interview with him."

Sara tensed slightly. "I don't think this is appropriate—"

"Dan says Bolingbrook is part of Jennifer's beat."

"Yes, but the speech is in Rosemont, which is part of my beat."

"Why do you need to interview Robert Clark? Why are you putting our advertising at risk?"

"Because I still have questions, and I—"

"It's one damn speech," said James, raising his voice. "Are you willing to risk one of our papers over a speech? We've already lost the *Romeoville Star*."

"If it's one speech then Robert shouldn't have a problem answering my questions," Sara replied.

"What questions?"

Sara didn't reply. How could she tell him about the mysterious voice on her taped interview with a village spokesperson? A voice she didn't remember hearing. A voice that dictated the article she was about to write.

"Look," sighed James. "If you need more work, there are plenty of other communities Dan can give you. Jennifer's built up quite a rapport with Mayor Clark. She's given us exclusive stories that help our circulation, and that have boosted our ad revenue. Bolingbrook accounts for a good portion of our ads. Robert knows that. He's not just the mayor of Bolingbrook. He's one of the most powerful politicians in the state. Have you seen his campaign fund numbers?"

"No, but—"

"Way out of proportion for a village like Bolingbrook. He's one of our biggest clients around election season. Hell, he could buy the *Star* with his fund and still have money left over. He also has pull with a lot of businesses — and not just in Bolingbrook." James sighed. "Sara, you need to focus on your communities. You've cultivated great sources. You have written some great stories, like the red light cameras in Des Plaines. That's where your focus needs to be, Sara. Not Bolingbrook."

"I have not neglected my communities," Sara protested. "I just need to ask Robert a few more questions about a story that affects Rosemont. Then I'll be done."

James shook his head. "Let me give you some advice, Sara. I'm not a reporter. You're a good reporter. However, I know the business side of journalism, and let me tell you, our industry is dying. The only paper in the black around here is the *Babbler*. They've got the weird tabloid market covered. There's no way I could publish the crap they publish and make a profit. Nor would you write for them."

Sara didn't answer.

"You have kids, right?"

"Yes," Sara replied. "Jacob and Monique."

"Before you go any further with your vendetta against Robert, you need to think about your children. Because if I lose any more money, there are going to be more layoffs. Now, because you did me a huge favor when you stopped me from hiring that college kid…"

"I merely warned you about his behavior at that convention. He could have been fixable."

"True, but we couldn't take that chance. I don't think you should be taking chances with your career. So, I would suggest you stop bothering Robert, focus on your communities, and in a few months, we might need an editor for the Northwest Region. Understand?"

***

Sara and her husband Peter sat on a bench in Knights of Columbus Park, watching Jacob and Monique playing on the swing set.

"Don't push your sister too high!" Peter yelled.

"Okay," Jacob replied. Monique laughed.

Peter's smile faded as he turned towards Sara.

"You're going to do what he says?"

"After I get the answers."

"Sara," replied Peter. "You can't afford to lose this job. Remember how long it took you to get hired by the *Star*?"

"I haven't forgotten," Sara replied.

"I think you should have been assigned to Bolingbrook," said Peter. "It's our home, but you didn't. Jennifer got it. You have to accept that."

"Peter," Sara snapped. "It's not about that."

"What is it about?"

"I want answers."

Peter gave Sara a befuddled look. "Answers? Since when did you care about digging for answers?"

"Since I heard that recorded voice." Sara looked around. "You heard it too."

"Yeah," Peter replied. "It was creepy, but maybe there's another explanation for it."

"Like what?"

"I don't know. Maybe it's from a previous recording. Maybe it was from another room. Maybe someone secretly added it to your tape as a joke. There has to be a reasonable explanation."

"If there is one, why won't the mayor provide it? Why are people threatening me?"

"I don't know, but it doesn't mean there's a mystery. Remember that convention you covered? The one that opposed the supernatural?"

"Habencon, yes?"

"You said they had a special term for investigating mysteries. What was it?"

"Debunk."

"Yeah. Maybe they can debunk this voice on the tape."

"Oh, they can debunk it," Sara replied. "I heard all kinds of debunking that weekend, but you know what I didn't hear. I didn't hear any of them trying to find out the truth. Most of them were sincere, but some of them—"

"Listen to yourself," Peter interrupted. "You're starting to sound like a *Babbler* reporter. What next? Aliens used the Illuminati's 5G network to plant a subliminal message on your tape recorder?"

"You're mocking me?" Sara loudly protested.

"Mommy?" asked Monique.

"Mommy's fine," Sara replied. "Keep playing." Sara paused for a moment then whispered to Peter. "You should be supporting me."

"I do support you," Peter replied in a firm but subdued tone. "I see what this is doing to you. You have to let it go. Think of our children."

***

Jacob slipped as he kicked the soccer ball. The goalie fell in front of the ball and let it roll into his chest.

"Good try, honey!" Sara called out from the bleachers. She enthusiastically clapped. "Next time you'll get it. Don't give up." She looked at the other parents sitting on the lower level. Peter was with Monique at her Martial Arts class. While she was proud of her progress in class, she preferred the fresh air while watching Jacob's team play and hoping to see his first goal.

A few minutes later, a man said, "Excuse me? Are you Sara?"

Sara looked up. The man was holding a worn-out notepad. His red polo shirt and blue jeans were both faded.

Sara replied: "Yes. You must be Mr. Watts?"

"Call me Don." Don motioned towards the bench. "May I?"

Sara nodded.

Don sat down. "Like I said, I got the copy of your tape. I had a colleague confirm its authenticity. You were very fortunate to get that recording. You impressed my editor and my publisher. You're with the *Star*, right?"

"Do you know what it is?"

Don nodded. "I do." He looked out at the field.

"And?" asked Sara.

"Which one is your son?"

"Why do you want to know?"

Don pulled a pen out of his shirt pocket. "Because there are consequences to knowing the answer." He opened his notepad. "Now, I don't care about my exes. My daughter's safe, but I hardly see her. Writing for the *Babbler* is interesting, but it can only keep you going for so long."

"Your point?"

"You have a family. Don't worry. I didn't dig too much. They probably know more."

"They?"

Don looked out at the field again. "They call Bolingbrook the pathway village for a reason. You're at a crossroads, so to speak. I can tell you that you're not imagining things and that I can take over the investigation. I don't think the *Star* would mind me stealing a story like this from them. The point is, you would go back to your family, and be done with it."

"Or?"

Don faced Sara. "Or I can extend an invitation to you. We're looking for a new editor, and you've caught our publisher's attention. You'd probably start off making more than I do. But you'd be starting down a dark, lonely, and possibly risky path. The good thing would be that Robert would tolerate you. The bad thing is almost no one will believe what you'll tell them. You will be stuck with us for the rest of your career. The worst part is, you'll attract the attention of forces and people far more dangerous than Robert. We have a pretty good survival rate, but some of us don't come out unscathed. And that doesn't include the Olson family. But then again. You'll have a far better view of how Bolingbrook and the rest of the world works." Don looked back at the field. "But you have to think about your children."

Sara glanced out at the field then locked her eyes on Don. "Don, right?"

"Yes."

"Don, when I was growing up, my parents were just happy I wasn't running with the wrong people. They didn't volunteer at my clubs or watch my games. They weren't bad. They were just too busy to think about me all the time. So, when I found out I was pregnant with Jacob, I promised myself that I would always think about my children. What I'm thinking right now is that there is something going on that I don't understand, and I need to understand it. I want to know what kind of world I'm sending my kids into, and I need to know what I can do to make it a better world. I'd rather be Cassandra than Koalemos. So, stop asking about my children, and start answering my questions."

Don sighed. "Very well. When do you want to meet the Olson family?"

The End

***

What happened after Miriam and Sara made their choices? Find out in *A Fire in the Shadows*.

Thank You

Thank you for reading this book. Please consider leaving a review at Goodreads and/or where you got a copy. Even a single-sentence review could encourage someone to get a copy.

For updates about my writing and bonus content, you can subscribe to my mailing list using the link below:

Mailing List: https://bolingbrookbabbler.com/mailing-list

Acknowledgments

Special thanks to wife and partner for her love and support over the years.

Thanks to the *Freethought Blogs* network for accepting me as a member, and for helping me grow as a person.

Finally, thanks to the many fans of the *Bolingbrook Babbler* blog. I'm honored to have entertained so many of you.

About William Brinkman

In William Brinkman's world, suburban sidewalks lead to secret conspiracies, emotional reckonings, and the occasional enraged weredeer. He writes urban fantasy with a blend of satire and heart, offering humanistic views of the real world through a supernatural lens. Since 1999, he's published the Bolingbrook Babbler blog, which inspired—but remains separate from—his fiction. His book, *A Fire in the Shadows*, made the short list for the 2024 Indieverse Award for Best Novella. A former Bolingbrook resident, William now lives in suburban Chicagoland with his wife and two cats.

For updates and a free eBook, *God to Smite Bolingbrook*, sign up for his newsletter.

https://bolingbrookbabbler.com/mailing-list

g

goodreads.com/author/show/5699299.William_Brinkman

f

facebook.com/bolingbrookbabbler/

♪

tiktok.com/@williambrinkmanbb

A FIRE
IN THE
SHADOWS

WILLIAM BRINKMAN

Preview of A Fire in the Shadows

Miriam was so desperate to escape her life that she accepted Matthew's offer. Even if it meant losing the ability to feel love and compassion. Miriam died to be reborn as Lydia, the vampire.

Lydia never expected to regain her ability to love and feel empathy. She didn't realize the danger it would put her in, or how lonely she would feel.

Her companions and blood family ridicule her for having "soft feelings." Lydia knows love can hurt, but love can be powerful. Just like fire.

From A Fire in the Shadows

Aurora kept talking, but Lydia focused on Sara and her companion, using her heightened sight and hearing. Both women were more interested in their conversation than their drinks.

"I think you should take over the weredeer story," said Sara.

"Me? I thought you assigned a freelance reporter."

"We lost touch with him. I don't think he ran away, and Wendy is still trying to figure out what happened. If he's still alive, we'll help him. But for now, we need someone to cover the story, and I would like you to take over."

"Okay, but it sounds dangerous."

"Not if we take a different approach. I'll give you the list of eyewitnesses to interview and you don't have to worry about getting photos. We'll use file photos instead. So that should minimize the risk."

Aurora stopped talking and frowned. She looked towards Sara's booth. "You know them?"

"The woman on the left is Sara. She's the *Babbler's* editor now. Not sure about the other woman."

"So, *that's* Sara."

"Yes. I saw her on my first patrol."

Aurora studied Lydia's face, then looked at Sara. "Are you rebounding already?" Lydia's focus remained solely on Sara as

Aurora gave her the side-eye. "She's a bit too old to twilight, don't you think?" asked Aurora.

"Twilighting" was when a vampire pretended to be in love with a young person as a joke. The *Twilight* series inspired both the fad and the term.

Lydia glared at her sister, who merely shrugged in response.

"It's true," Aurora replied. "She looks too old. The one on the right is a better target."

"Target? Really, Aurora?"

"Okay. Why Sara then?"

Lydia shook her head, then returned her attention to Sara once more. She was telling a story about a rare book collector she met in Chicago. Lydia kept her focus on Sara. "You wouldn't understand."

"Let me guess, then." Aurora squinted at Sara for a moment. "Is it the hair? You just want to reach out and touch it? Is it her nails? Her boobs? Her chocolate—"

"She's not food," snapped Lydia.

"You're right. We would drink her blood, not eat her. Good point."

Lydia snarled. "Drop it, Aurora."

"After you explain why you want to twilight an adult."

Lydia sighed. "I don't want to twilight her. You wouldn't understand."

"Try me."

Lydia looked back at Sara. She found some people's faces alluring, but could never articulate the characteristics she desired. Lydia felt that desire when she looked at Sara's face. But it wasn't just physical attraction. The way Sara cared about her companion brought back memories from her childhood. When their father was in his study, Miriam and her sister would spend time with their cats. Her sister taught Miriam about feline care, like the right way to hold a cat, and the best games to play with them. In those moments, her caring voice warmed Miriam's heart and helped her feel safe. Just like Sara's voice was making her feel. "She feels like... home."

Aurora gave Lydia a quizzical look. "Home?" She squinted as she scanned Sara, as if she was trying to see what Lydia was seeing.

"I said you wouldn't understand."

Lydia shifted her focus back to Sara. Home is the right word, she thought.

THE RIFT

Preview of The Rift

Tom Larsen had everything a skeptic blogger could want: loyal followers, a steady stream of income, and multiple outlets. To the skeptic community, he's one of the brave heroes defending the movement against a takeover attempt by "radical feminists" like podcaster Jamie Kyle. But deep down inside, Tom is still fuming over a video Jamie posted about him.

When Tom finds out that Jamie and the other feminist skeptics are going to hold a congress in his hometown of Bolingbrook, he sees a chance to get his revenge. He just needs one media outlet to let him cover the Congress.

Unfortunately, the only media organization willing to meet with him is the *Bolingbrook Babbler*. Tom's hometown tabloid is infamous for its sensational articles about an alien base under Bolingbrook, and cryptids roaming the neighboring forest preserves. The *Babbler* is the anthesis of everything the skeptical movement stands for. But desperate times call for desperate measures...

The Rift: Chapter 3

"The mission of skeptical organizations is to promote skepticism. Anything else is mission drift."
—@thativancabot

As Tom approached the strip malls along Barber's Corner in his blue Toyota Echo, he could make out the words *Bolingbrook Babbler* among the red brick buildings. The gray concrete slab roofs brought World War II bunkers to mind. Across Route 53, he could see the new Portillo's building and the businesses that replaced the East Boughton Drive Jewel-Osco store where his parents used to shop.

Tom made a left turn on the access road. After a short drive, he turned into the parking lot and soon found himself in front of the *Babbler's* office. Two days ago, he never would have imagined himself here.

After the board meeting, still high from his public comments, Tom had approached the village clerk, thinking she would give him a form to fill out to become a registered Bolingbrook media outlet. Instead, she recorded his information and said she had a backlog of applications to approve. Tom suspected she wasn't telling him the truth. She suggested Tom ask one of the registered outlets to sponsor him. Otherwise, he could be waiting at least a month.

The drive home had been one of the worst car trips he'd taken with his parents since they went to Malta, Illinois and got lost in the corn maze. This time his parents ceaselessly grilled him on his remarks. When they offered to pay for him to see a therapist, Tom refused. As his parents kept insisting he needed help, Tom wondered why his mother, whom he considered a rational feminist, didn't understand.

The next day had only made matters worse. He emailed all the suburban newspapers, asking if any were interested in a story about the Humanist Heart congress. As a joke, he even emailed a pitch to the *Babbler*, penning a fake story in their style. He remembered laughing as he emailed them. Surely, he thought, at least one serious news outlet would accept his pitch. How could they not cover a feminist invasion of suburbia?

None of the area papers were interested—one editor even offered to pray for him. Well, almost none. The editor of the *Babbler* had been interested, and insisted on meeting in person.

Tom stood at the front door. Painted on the glass were the words: *Bolingbrook's first and only true tabloid since 1965.* Tom let out a sigh and trudged in.

Entering a room of brown cubicles, Tom heard some members of staff talking on the phone, while others typed away at their keyboards. A front counter and two side counters separated the reception area from the newsroom. Framed copies of old *Babbler* issues lined the walls. To his far left, he saw a door and made out the word "Publisher." *Probably the only actual office in this building.*

Tom noticed a woman at an open-air desk. She was wearing a gray textured t-shirt and faded jeans. Tom thought she looked familiar, but couldn't recall why.

The woman looked up from her computer. "Can I help you?"

"I have a meeting with Sara," Tom replied.

"You must be Tom." She stood up and walked towards the counter. "I'm Wendy Onofrey. Pleased to meet you." Tom shook her hand. "Sara got called into a meeting with our publisher. Something about a job applicant." Wendy lifted the hinged part of the counter and opened a small door. "You can wait back here with me."

As Tom walked into the news area, Wendy motioned for him to sit in a chair by her desk.

"You wouldn't happen to be that job applicant?"

Tom shook his head. "Just submitting a piece. If it goes well, maybe she'll let me cover a special event at the Golf Club."

"Humanist Heart?"

Tom raised his eyebrows. "You've heard of them?"

"Of course," Wendy replied. "It's our job to know what's going on in Bolingbrook."

Tom fought the urge to make a snarky remark as he sat down. "I hope she'll let me cover it."

Wendy nodded. "If you do, investigate why they're holding it here. The Golf Club doesn't exactly scream social justice. Plus, Robert doesn't strike me as one of them. Though I think the official story is right about one thing: It would be the safest place. It is the secondary command center for Bolingbrook."

"Oh. I think I remember reading about that."

"A reader," Wendy replied. "I like that."

"Well—"

"Lots of residents just glance at our covers. I like the ones who take the time to read our articles."

Tom politely nodded, wondering when Sara's meeting would end.

Wendy continued. "Anyway. It'll be interesting to see what happens. Like I said, it's the safest place in Illinois, next to Clow Base, of course. Considering they found a bomb at the last location, they'll need the protection."

Tom chuckled. "I guess the village will protect them while they conspire against the skeptical movement."

Wendy shook her head. "Actually, that's not the point of this meeting. From what I've read, they're divided between the forum-only faction and the non-profit faction. So, this is really a congress about the future of the group. Do they stick with being an Internet space for progressive skeptics, or do they become a progressive version of the Habenstein Society? They also need to decide if they want to work with other groups. Since some of them will have observers there, it should be a lively event."

"I expect it will be. All the drama should interest your readers."

Wendy looked closer at Tom, then raised her finger. "Say, did you used to write a blog?"

"Still do. It's called *Skeptical Hurricane*."

"Oh." Wendy looked uncomfortable as she leaned away. "I remember when it was *Skeptical Butterfly*."

Tom failed to contain his surprise.

"Back when I posted on the Habenstein Society's forums," said Wendy, "I remember seeing a lot of links to your posts. I enjoyed reading them."

Tom furrowed his brow. "You used to be a skeptic?"

"Still am."

"You are?" Tom stumbled. "I didn't expect..."

"To find a skeptic here? Actually, this is the best place for a skeptic. I've learned more here than I ever did in the skeptical movement."

"You left the movement?"

"It left me."

"Onofrey? Are you related—"

"To the guy who trolls skeptics? Yes. We used to be identical."

"Oh," Tom replied.

The back door opened. A man and woman walked in, carrying bags and drinks from Portillo's.

"Lunchtime!" said the woman, who wore a black pantsuit and appeared to be close to Tom's age. Tom admired her copper hair for a moment, then turned his attention back to Wendy.

"Perfect," Wendy replied, then looked at Tom. "Portillo's day is one of the few perks we have."

Other staff members emerged from the cubicles. While the man placed most of the bags on a table, the woman approached with a bag marked for Wendy. Wendy accepted it, and the woman glanced at the publisher's office.

"They're still meeting?"

"Yep," Wendy replied. "I think he wasn't too pleased. Especially if he called Sara in."

The woman stared at the door for a few moments, then faced Wendy. "They should be done soon. Oh, your friend says thanks for lunch. He's seen two rifts this week."

"Thanks. I'll take care of it."

"Sure." The woman noticed Tom and stepped closer. "Have we met?"

"I don't think so."

"Excuse me," said Wendy. "I forgot my manners. Tom, this is Jenna Olson, our sales representative, and one of our resident psychics."

Jenna smiled. "Actually, I prefer the term percipient."

"Jenna," Wendy continued, "This is Tom. He wants to submit a piece."

"Oh!" said Jenna. "So, what's your article about?"

"You're asking?" said Tom.

"Yes?" Jenna replied.

"You're the psychic." Tom closed his eyes and imagined the answer. When he opened them, he saw Jenna frowning at him.

"That was rude," she said. "You shouldn't test someone without asking. And if you're going to, do the right test, because I have precognition, not telepathy."

"My apologies," Tom sarcastically replied. "I don't normally hang out with precogs."

"Don't mention that movie."

"Noted. So, what am I doing next week?"

Jenna glared at Tom for a moment, then her face relaxed. She tilted her head, then stepped closer, squinting her eyes for a few moments before straightening her posture and stepping back.

"That's odd," she said. "It seems like you're not doing anything next week."

"Nothing?"

"Nothing. Wait." She tilted her head again. "Something about you feels off."

"Off?" Tom asked. "Ah. I get it. You just need my credit card number to fine tune your vision."

"No," Jenna snapped.

"Something *is* wrong," added Wendy. "She should see something, even if you're dead next week."

"Yet I don't see or sense anything about you," said Jenna. "You're full of surprises, Tom."

"I suppose," Tom answered. "Or maybe you know better than to try a cold reading—"

"Really?" Jenna replied, frowning.

"She isn't a cold reader," said Wendy. "Notice she didn't flood you with questions."

"But she gave a vague answer."

"I was very specific," protested Jenna.

"'Nothing' is a specific answer?"

"Yes."

"So I'm going to cease to exist next week?"

Wendy shook her head. "More likely her brain can't process what she's seeing."

"Process?"

"Let me show you." Wendy picked up a business card and wrote Tom's name, placed the card in her hand, then turned both her palms down on the desk. "Where's the card?"

"Your other hand?"

Wendy showed Tom both of her empty palms. "Our brains make mistakes." She pulled the card out of her desk drawer and placed it in front of Tom. He saw his name written on it. "Our brains are evolved to make assumptions, and some of those assumptions are wrong—you were fooled by my misdirection. Jenna sees parts of the future, but can't always tell what she's looking at."

Tom reluctantly nodded.

"Reese taught me that trick," said Wendy. "If you want to be published in the *Babbler*, you really should be more open-minded."

Tom felt his face warm with embarrassment. He still didn't believe Jenna was a psychic, but he needed access to the congress.

"While I have questions," Tom sighed. "I'm sorry you were hurt by how I asked them."

"You're sorry I was offended?" asked Jenna.

"Yes," said Tom. He decided humor might lighten things. "I'm sorry, and I promise to never introduce you to Anti-Psychic Kitty."

"Tom," said Wendy. "Anti-Psychic Kitty almost killed her father."

"Seriously? The CAS's mascot? How?"

"That is a *very* long story," came a new voice. Tom turned and saw a Black woman in her late thirties wearing a white blouse with gray slacks. "Which my staff don't have time to tell because we have *an issue. To finish.*"

Tom stood up. "I'm—"

"I know who you are. Sara Langston, editor. We have a lot to talk about." She offered her hand, shaking Tom's firmly, then motioned for him to follow.

Jenna approached Tom. "Before you go, there's one thing I should tell you. Bolingbrook is known as the Pathway Village. Don't be afraid to change paths."

Jenna smiled before returning to Wendy's desk.

Tom gave Jenna a puzzled look, then followed Sara into her cubicle. The divider walls were bare, but behind the desk was a small bookshelf. On top of it were pictures he assumed were of her husband and daughter. Two books stood out to Tom: a worn copy of a guide to haunted places in Chicago, and one titled *Blood in the Wind: The Secret History of Chicagoland's Vampire Kingdoms and Free Territories.*

Sara motioned towards the chair in front of her desk. Tom sat and placed a printout of his article in front of her. For the first time since college, an editor was about to review his writing. Sara sat down, clicked her wireless mouse, and turned her attention to her screen. Tom removed a pen from his shirt pocket and set it next to the printout.

"You aren't making my job easy," said Sara.

"Oh?"

"Our publisher has concerns about printing anything by you. Insulting his granddaughter didn't help your case."

Tom suddenly felt like he'd swallowed a black hole. The Olson family owned the *Babbler*. He should have recognized Jenna's last name.

"Oh God," Tom heard himself whisper. "I can apologize right now. It's just—um. I'm sorry. It won't happen again."

"Good," Sara replied. "Considering Jenna's visions are one reason I invited you here, I hope you'll show her more respect."

"I will," Tom blurted out.

"That's good to hear. You can take a minute."

"Thank you," said Tom as he tried to calm himself down. After a few deep breaths, he relaxed. "I'm ready."

"Good. So, let's start with your sample story."

Tom felt his confidence return. "You're welcome to publish it, and if you need any minor corrections—"

"You made this up."

Tom waited several uncomfortable moments for Sara to continue. She continued to glare at him.

Say something.

"And?" asked Tom.

Sara leaned towards him. "You wrote a piece of fiction. A sloppy piece of fiction. We don't print fiction here."

Tom's jaw dropped. *How can I be blowing this?*

"Look at your story," said Sara. "It's about Gray-type aliens. There's no such thing as Grays. Then you brought Bigfoot into it. Bolingbrook doesn't have a Bigfoot population. Even if it did, aliens don't carry away Bigfoot corpses. They turn to dust. I also know you didn't interview any aliens. That's just the first paragraph." Tom gulped as Sara continued. "I could go on, but let me get to the point: We're not a literary magazine and we don't print fiction."

"Come on," Tom protested. "If I'm guilty of anything, it's not paying close attention to your recent stories. I'll read some more—"

"I said we don't publish fiction."

"But everyone in Bolingbrook knows your stories aren't real. *I* know they're not real. I grew up here. I've seen Hidden Lakes. I've walked the trails. We laugh at your articles because we know they're not real. You can't criticize me because my story is fiction when everything the *Babbler*'s ever published is fictional. And that's beside the point—I want to write about something real!"

Sara shook her head. "Maybe if I'd spent as many years among skeptics as you, I wouldn't think twice about submitting this. Maybe I'd feel like pranking the *Babbler* was serving humanity. But let me assure you, Tom. All the articles we publish are about something real."

Tom blinked. "Are you seriously trying to tell me you believe everything you publish?"

Sara leaned back in her chair and paused for a moment. "Of course I do. My name is on the masthead. Before I worked here, I thought the stories were fiction. But let's just say after I had a run-in with the men in blue, I became more open-minded. That nearly got me fired from my previous paper, but I wanted to know the truth. So, I feel very fortunate to work for the *Babbler*. Our content may seem like a joke to you, but we make sure we thoroughly research stories before publishing them. Do you believe me now?"

Tom considered the possibilities. "I... understand that you believe what you publish."

"That's a good start."

Time to recover.

"So, I apologize for writing a fiction piece. I didn't know how committed you and your staff are to reporting what you believe is the truth. I hope I can make up for it by writing a story—a real story—for you. Let me tell you what I have to offer."

"I'm listening," said Sara.

"Let's start with my YouTube channel."

"Let's not."

Tom swallowed.

Sara continued. "Let's talk about your blog. Back when it was *Skeptical Butterfly*, you did a good job. You were more thorough than most skeptics, even though you toed the party line. Then once your pass at Jamie Kyle backfired, you—"

"*You!*" Tom looked closer at Sara. His eyes widened. "You were at our table that night."

"I was. When I saw Jamie's video, it was obvious who she was talking about."

"You told my editor."

"Yes, but it wasn't my goal to get you fired. I wanted her to give you a warning. Our publisher, however, either feared a lawsuit or wanted an excuse to let you go. Were you aware of the layoffs that followed your release?"

Tom stood up and turned.

"I can get you into the Golf Club."

Tom stopped as desperation overpowered his anger. He turned and faced Sara, who was still sitting at her desk.

"I'm working on securing a press pass for the congress. If we don't get one, we have the connections necessary to get someone in undercover. Wendy has the background to cover the congress, but she's responsible for the layout and the website. I can't risk putting her out in the field."

"I see your point."

Sara continued. "I've looked at the stories you wrote in college. You were an excellent investigative journalist. That article on corruption in UIC's student government? Impressive."

"Thank you?" Tom replied, hesitant.

"Not every reporter can say they forced a politician to leave the country. You know where he is now?"

"I heard he's running a casino for the Russian mob."

"That's my understanding. It takes courage to do investigative journalism."

"I guess," Tom replied.

"But I have a question. Your blog says you're a man going your own way. Correct?"

"Basically."

"So why not keep going? You have a successful blog and podcast with thousands of followers. You're a leader in your movement, even if you don't think of yourself as one. Why do you have to go to this meeting? I won't send you there if you're just going to harass Jamie."

Tom's heart sped up again. "I'm not! This is—"

"Good. Sit down."

Tom sat down.

"What do you know about weredeer?"

***

Tom sighed as he drove east. It was after 11 PM, and to the north, he could just make out the old landfill mound—Mount Bolingbrook, as he liked to call it. To the south, he could see the fence securing the Elmhurst-Chicago quarry. *Another uneventful night.*

He'd read about weredeer in the *Babbler,* and unfortunately still remembered key details. They were like werewolves, except their animal phenotype was a deer. They could shift into one of three forms: humanoid, deer, and alpha. As Sara had reminded him, a weredeer in its alpha form could hold its own in a fight with a dire wolf. She had also reminded him they couldn't mate with each other. While they could mate with normal deer, some weredeer obsessively focused on mating with humans.

Sara had also claimed that there were two local factions of weredeer: suburban and feral. In the 1990s, the suburban weredeer, persuaded by the Bolingbrook Jaycees, agreed to abide by traditional human courtship customs, even if it reduced the chance of producing weredeer born from humans. In exchange, the village would recognize them as Bolingbrook residents. A minority rejected the deal. Not wanting to be hunted by the village's Department of Paranormal Affairs, the feral weredeer retreated to the forest preserves, pledging only to mate with deer.

As a teenager, Tom remembered laughing at the *Babbler's* blurry photos of weredeer in their alpha form. If anyone showed him a blurry photo of Bigfoot, Tom would counter by showing them a blurry photo of a weredeer. Why, Tom would ask, did people believe in Bigfoot but not weredeer, despite there being more photographic evidence for the latter? Some of his classmates told him he was an asshole, while others just called him Bolingbrook High's official class skeptic.

Now the class skeptic was driving down Royce Road trying to find a creature that only existed on the pages of the *Babbler*. According to Sara, hundreds of feral weredeer from around the country were gathering for unknown reasons in the nearby woods. His assignment was to investigate.

This was how Tom had spent most of the week. He'd interviewed all the people on Sara's list of weredeer eyewitnesses. Most sounded sincere, but no one had caught an unambiguous view of a weredeer. A few claimed to have seen something in the woods that moved too fast to be a normal deer. One witness said she'd been walking towards Hidden Lakes Historic Trout Farm and "heard a foreign-sounding voice." Then, she said, a deer had jumped out of the woods, and "glared" at her.

The field skepticism workshops at Habencon portrayed fieldwork as informative, exciting, and short. Old Man Jake from the Committee for Humanism and Skepticism had bragged about all the new skills he'd learned from his investigations, like how to break a board with his hands. The "ghost couple" from France had claimed they could debunk any haunted site in a single night. The Open Investigations Team had countless funny videos debunking psychics. Tom wasn't learning anything, he wasn't having fun, and wasn't even close to resolving the "weredeer mystery." Exhausted and frustrated, he took comfort in knowing that he only had one more area to check out before he could go to bed. Fortunately, it was close to his apartment.

From his phone, which was plugged into the Echo's stereo, Trevor DeBruin's voice jolted Tom back to the present. "It is time to put away the beliefs that now drive feminism," he said. "Time for a philosophy that celebrates sexuality instead of shaming men. Time for a society that does not favor females. If saying so makes us bigots in the eyes of the headless humanists, then so be it. We know the truth." Tom smiled as he reached the intersection of Royce and Route 53.

How many times would he have to investigate weredeer sightings before Wendy and Sara believed they weren't real? It was amazing how the *Babbler's* staff were so committed to its worldview. How could Wendy believe it as well? Having read the same books and followed the same blogs as Tom, even attended conventions years before him, how could she possibly believe in the paranormal?

When Tom reached the intersection of North Ashbury and Boughton, he turned right. Despite his boredom, Tom intently scanned the neighborhood as he drove south. The houses were a mix of brick ranch homes and two-story houses with white vinyl siding. Evenly spaced adolescent trees lined the parkway. If there were deer or weredeer in the area, they weren't in anyone's yards. Tom suspected that in thirty to fifty years, the street would look like it had a green canopy. His friends from Chicago complained that neighborhoods like these made Bolingbrook feel cookie-cutter, but driving through these subdivisions made Tom feel like he was home.

A few minutes later, movement to the right caught Tom's attention. He slowed down and turned the car slightly so its headlights would illuminate the scene. Ahead, he recognized a white-tailed stag with four points on each antler. The buck, its back turned towards Tom, had its front legs perched on a windowsill. It looked strong, like one of the many airbrushed deer photos he saw in magazines and on hunting websites. Right now, it appeared to be sniffing the window. Tom opened the glove compartment, pulling out his flashlight after a few seconds of fumbling and flicking it on. To his relief, the light came on.

Tom drove several feet forward; the deer was now directly to his right. He pointed the flashlight at the buck, which dropped from the window and turned to face him. Tom shone the light at its face. The deer's eyes reflected the white glare, and Tom cursed himself for even entertaining the thought that this was more than a very curious deer. Tom turned off the flashlight, but instead of vanishing, the glow in the creature's eyes turned to electric blue.

Tom's muscles tensed, his eyelids peeling back as if by force, and his right foot instinctively slammed on the accelerator. The Echo's engine roared to life as it sped away from the beast. Tom dropped the flashlight and clenched the steering wheel, hands trembling. In the rearview mirror, he saw the deer's fiery eyes.

Instinctively, Tom turned left onto Independence Lane, tires barely gripping the road. Soon, the houses obscured his view of the deer. After two blocks, Tom slammed on the brakes and struggled to catch his breath, heart still racing. Tom noticed Trevor's video still playing on his phone.

"I'm going to be joining protesters at Humanist Heart International's congress," came Trevor's voice. Tom smiled and relaxed, reaching down to recover his phone from the floor. "As my long-time followers know, I'm going, even if the area isn't wheelchair accessible. What about the rest of you sitting on the fence? I'm sure most of you have two working legs. What's your excuse?"

Tom placed his phone in the passenger seat and looked up. In the rearview mirror, Tom glimpsed a large dark shape descending from the sky. A moment later, it landed on top of a parked car with a loud crash. The landing crushed the roof of the car, setting off its alarm. Tom closed his eyes and shook his head, then turned to look through the rear window.

What looked like an alpha deer stood on top of the car, pummeling the hood. Each punch dented the metal like a jackhammer. If it was an alpha, the photos Tom had seen didn't convey their actual size. The points of its antlers looked razor sharp, its front legs now resembling a gorilla's arms, hind legs sporting talons instead of hooves. It stopped punching and opened its hands, revealing clawed fingers that glistened in the streetlights. The creature swiped at the car's hood, shredding it like cardboard and tossing it away. The hood swam through the air before crashing through a neighboring home's windows.

The weredeer looked towards Tom's car, its eyes still fiery blue. It roared in Tom's direction, revealing a set of shark-like teeth while shaking the Echo.

Tom slammed on the accelerator. The car struggled to pick up speed, while the creature charged on its hands and feet, biting down seconds later into the car's trunk. Over Trevor's voice, Tom could hear the steel being ripped off. In the mirror, he saw the creature with a sizable chunk of blue metal in its mouth. It slowed down as it chewed.

Tom shifted the car into fifth, continuing to gather speed. He sped past the stop sign as the road merged with North Ashbury. Behind him, the creature spit out the remaining scraps of metal and resumed its pursuit. All the other side streets in this direction were dead ends, Tom remembered: his only hope of escape was to get back to Boughton. The Echo was now up to highway speed and the weredeer was still gaining. Tom pressed the accelerator against the floor. *It has to break off at some point.*

The Echo's tires squealed as the road curved, and the weredeer slowed slightly as it made the turn, then resumed closing in. As the road meandered, the Echo barely held onto the pavement, while the weredeer cut the distance by moving straight. Boughton was now visible and only seconds away. Though the traffic was light, he knew making a left turn at this speed would be impossible. The weredeer was only inches behind.

Tom spun the steering wheel, desperately attempting a hard right onto Boughton. As he heard a car horn blaring at him, he closed his eyes. Instead of a collision, he heard the approaching car crash into the weredeer. Before the outside world tilted, Tom opened his eyes and glimpsed the creature tumbling to the ground in the rearview mirror.

***

What happens next? Get The Rift: A Bolingbrook Babbler Story *to find out.*

Also By William Brinkman

The Bolingbrook Babbler Stories

- *Pathways to Bolingbrook: A Bolingbrook Babbler Story* Book 1(2021)

- *A Fire in the Shadows: A Bolingbrook Babbler Story Book 1.5 (2023)*

- *The Rift: A Bolingbrook Babbler Story* Book 2 (2022)

- *Revenge of the Phantom Press: A Bolingbrook Babbler Story* Book 3 (2026)

Web Fiction Collection

- God to Smite Bolingbrook (2023)

Demon: The Fallen (White Wolf Studios)

- *Demon: The Fallen* (2002)

- *Saviors and Destroyers* "Broken Bonds" (2003)

- *Damned and Deceived* "The Good Soldier" (2003)